The HEALING BOOK

Place a Special
Photo Here

Facing the Death—and Celebrating the Life—of Someone You Love

by Ellen Sabin

and _____

WRITE YOUR NAME HERE

WATERING CAN® PRESS
www.wateringcanpress.com

WATERING CAN®

Growing Kids with Character

When you care about things and nurture them,
they will grow healthy, strong, and happy, and in turn,
they will make the world a better place.

Text and illustrations © 2006 by Ellen Sabin

WATERING CAN is a registered trademark of Ellen Sabin.

Written by Ellen Sabin
Illustrated by Kerren Barbas
Designed by Heather Zschock

ISBN-10: 0-9759868-3-X
ISBN-13: 978-0-9759868-3-7
Printed in China
By Best Tri Colour Printing and Packaging, Ltd.

Website address: www.wateringcanpress.com

Dear _____,

It can be very hard and confusing when someone you love dies.

You may have many questions or feel many different things. Talking about your feelings, asking questions, and remembering the person who died can help you feel better.

The **HEALING BOOK** gives you a place to write about those feelings, questions, and thoughts.

You can also use this book to remember the person you lost and all the wonderful things that make him or her so special to you. You can write these things down and make a scrapbook to cherish and celebrate that special person.

I am giving you this book because you are so special to me!

From, _____

A Note from Ellen

I wrote this book for my nieces and nephews the summer my family faced several deaths. I also wrote it for myself. I saw many books that focused on the psychology of death and grieving—the stages, stories, or instructions. These books have their place, but I was looking for something else.

The Healing Book arose because I simply felt sad and, from the bottom of my heart, missed the people I lost. I needed to feel the loss, express it, and write about it. I also needed to spend time recalling my love, my experiences, and my life with them in it. That's what felt right to me and that's what helped me the most. It's also what helped me start thinking about ways to feel better and heal.

I hope you, or those who you share this book with, find as much comfort in these pages as I did in writing them.

A NOTE TO ADULTS

We know that dealing with the death of a loved one is difficult for everyone.
It is especially hard for children.

When children are faced with a death, they can be confused and overwhelmed.

The Healing Book helps children to cope with this challenge by allowing them to explore their feelings,
confront their concerns, and identify their questions.

This book also invites children to create a memorial, in the form of a scrapbook,
where they can hold positive memories that they can cherish for the rest of their lives.

Adults can help children use THE HEALING BOOK to grow through their grief.

Be mindful and responsive to the questions children ask—
your openness will help them heal.

Even if children have the skills to read this book independently,
they will likely benefit most if you read through the book with them.

Adults can also call upon the assistance of therapists or other professionals
for children or members of their families to further facilitate
understanding, communication, grieving, and healing.

Table of Contents

What is
The HEALING BOOK?

A lot of things can happen when someone you love dies:

- You may have many different feelings or emotions.
- You may really miss the person and wish that you could see and talk to him or her again.
- Your family, friends, or other people around you may also be upset or sad.
- There may have been a funeral or other types of events after the death.
- Sometimes it will mean that there are a lot of things changing around you.

This book is for you.

It will let you think about how you feel and give you a way to express those feelings.

It will offer you a place to write down your questions and concerns about death, funerals, change, and anything else that is important to you.

It will give you ideas about things you can do that will make you feel a little better when you are sad and upset.

It will give you a chance to record your memories and all the special things about the person who died. You can create a scrapbook for these memories that will help you keep him or her in your heart and thoughts for the rest of your life.

How does The HEALING BOOK work?

When someone you care about dies, you go through a process called grieving. All of the different feelings in your heart, your head, and in your body are parts of grieving. Grieving can be hard, but it is very normal. It is also the way that you begin to heal. This HEALING BOOK is your personal book to help you grieve and feel better.

First You explore your thoughts and feelings about losing someone you love.

Then You think about the questions you have about death, funerals, or the person who died. You can write those questions down and then talk to friends and family about them.

Next You get to spend time remembering the person who died and thinking about all the special and unique things about him or her. By writing these things down, you can create a scrapbook to hold your memories and keep this person in your heart forever.

Then You can find things to do that will help make you feel better when you are sad or upset.

Remember:

This is YOUR book and you can use it however YOU want!

You can write in it, draw pictures, keep a journal,
and collect your thoughts.

- Sometimes you may want to spend a lot of time thinking about your feelings and remembering the person who died. At those times, using this book might make you feel better.

  Other times, thinking and remembering might feel too difficult, so you might want to put your book down and think about something else or do other things.

- You can do as much or as little of the book as you feel like doing. You might want to look through the whole book or you might want to skip around and just do some parts. You can also put it away and take it out again in a few days, weeks, or months from now.

- You can use this book on your own or you can share it with family, friends, teachers, or other special people in your life.

So, take your time and use your
HEALING BOOK when and how you want!

How do You FEEL?

People have all sorts of different feelings when someone they love dies.

It is important to know that:

Whatever you are feeling is OK.

and

You might have a bunch of different feelings.

and

You might not be sure exactly what you are feeling,
but you might want to cry, yell, sleep, sit quietly,
or run around, and that's OK, too.

and

Your feelings will change—sometimes quickly
and sometimes not so quickly.

How do you feel?

The words below describe some of the ways people might feel after someone they love dies. Have you felt any of these things since the person you love died?

Circle any of the words that describe how you have felt.

embarrassed

cheated

sad

weird

mad

CONFUSED

ignored

left alone

tired

WORRIED

stupid

quiet

guilty

sick

OK

not sure

jealous

SCARED

lost

brave

loved

relieved

angry

Are there other words that describe how you have felt? If so, you can write them here:

Look at the words that you circled or wrote down.
Now pick four of those words and write down more about each feeling.

WORD:

When do you feel that way?

What makes you feel that way?

What do you do when you feel that way?

WORD:

When do you feel that way?

What makes you feel that way?

What do you do when you feel that way?

WORD:

When do you feel that way?

What makes you feel that way?

What do you do when you feel that way?

WORD:

When do you feel that way?

What makes you feel that way?

What do you do when you feel that way?

A Roller Coaster of Feelings

Some people compare their feelings after someone dies to being on a roller coaster because they have so many ups and downs. Grieving can feel like hard work, and when you work hard, you may feel tired!

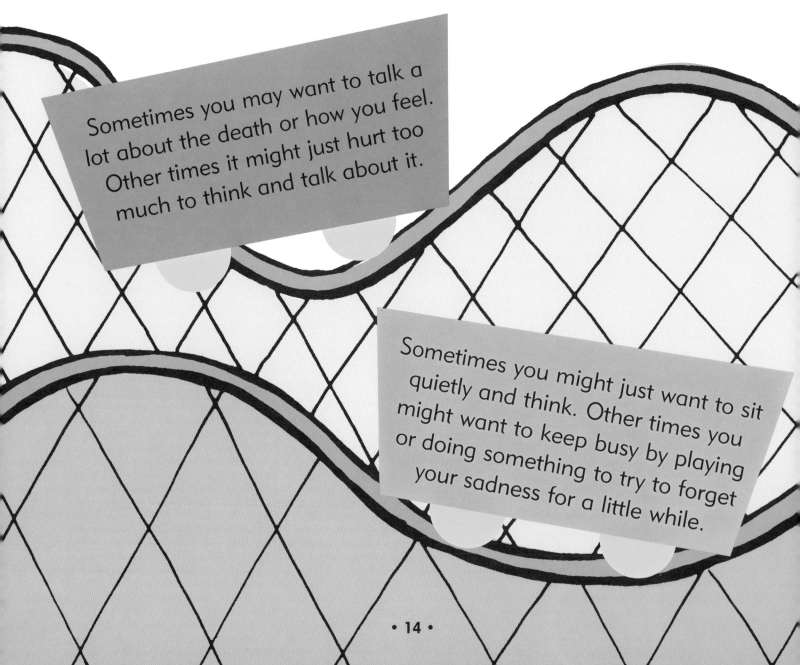

Sometimes you may want to talk a lot about the death or how you feel. Other times it might just hurt too much to think and talk about it.

Sometimes you might just want to sit quietly and think. Other times you might want to keep busy by playing or doing something to try to forget your sadness for a little while.

Sometimes you might want to be alone. Other times you might want to be around people.

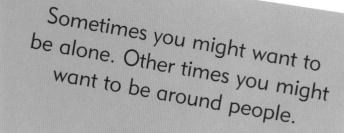

Sometimes you may have happy thoughts and memories about the person who died. Other times you might feel angry with him or her.

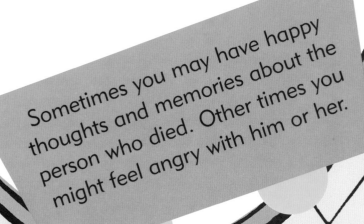

Sometimes it might seem like other people understand how you are feeling. Other times people might seem to be saying all the wrong things to you.

Feelings Can Hurt

Losing someone who is important to you can really make your heart hurt—but it can also make your body hurt, too.

It's normal for your body to react when someone dies. Some people get stomachaches. Other people might get headaches or feel like they can't think straight.

You can write how you've been feeling here:

Nighttime can be especially hard after someone you know dies. Some nights, it might take you an extra-long time to fall asleep, while other nights (and days) you might feel so tired that you have a hard time staying awake.

When you do fall asleep you might have nice dreams about the person who died, bad dreams, or no dreams at all.

How have you been sleeping? Have you had any dreams? You can write about them here:

Remember, grieving is hard work for the mind and body.

What can you do when you have strong feelings?

Sometimes your feelings may get very strong. You may feel very sad, very mad, or very upset. When your feelings are strong, there are things you can do to help make yourself feel better.

Here are some examples of things you can do to help deal with your strong feelings. Remember, everyone reacts differently, but some of these things might feel right to you.

Take care of yourself:

- Drink lots of water
- Don't forget to eat
- If you are tired, rest
- Talk to family or friends when you need to

What else seems healthy to you?

Activities to try:

- Running, swimming, biking
- Punching a pillow
- Playing with a friend
- Writing, drawing, thinking

What other activities might help you feel better?

Your QUESTIONS
About Death

People often feel confused about death.

Maybe you are wondering ...

...how or why people die.

...what happens when someone dies.

...how to act or feel.

One of the best things to do when you are confused is to ask questions.

You may not learn the answer to every single question, but by talking about things, you might start feeling a little less confused.

Are you scared about something now?

Sometimes people are afraid of things that they don't understand.
It's normal to feel more sensitive after someone dies.
If you feel scared about anything, write about it here:

Are you confused about any of the thoughts or feelings you are having?

Some people wonder why they sometimes feel happy when they think they should be just upset. Some people get confused because they feel angry with the person who died at the same time that they feel sad. People get confused about different things. Write about any thoughts or feelings that confuse you here:

After you write down your thoughts, you might want to
share them with a family member, friend, or teacher.

Are you confused about how other people around you are feeling or acting?

When some people grieve, they appear mad when they're really just sad. Some want to talk and others get really quiet. It's easy to misunderstand other people's actions when they are grieving. If you are upset or confused by how others are acting, write about it here:

....

....

....

Is there anything that you want to know about how the person you love died?

You can write those questions here:

....

....

....

It's not always easy to talk about your feelings,
but it often helps if you do.

The Funeral or Other Events

After someone dies, there may be a lot happening around you.

Sometimes there are a lot of people around. They may come to visit and offer their support. They may bring flowers, food, or cards to show they are thinking about you.

Often other people you love are sad. They may be acting differently because they are having strong feelings, too.

Most likely there will be a funeral or other events where people gather to say good-bye to the person who died.

People often feel differently about these events.

It makes some people glad to be around others during these times. But some people prefer to be alone. Some people find comfort in the funeral or events, but others do not.

Some families include children in all of the events, while other families don't.

Whatever is going on is new and different, and if you are not sure how to act or feel, that's OK.

Do you have any questions about the funeral or other events that happen when someone dies?

Write them here.

....

....

....

....

....

How do you feel about these events?

Did you go to them? If so, you can write about what happened and how those things made you feel. If you didn't participate in the events, you can write about how that made you feel.

....

....

....

....

....

People believe different things about death.

Are you curious or confused about what happens to a person after they die?

Doctors will explain that when someone dies, their body stops working. But people often wonder what happens to someone *after* they die.

Often, people's religious or cultural beliefs will affect what they think happens after someone dies. Some people believe that when a person dies he or she has a soul that lives on forever. Other people think that a person may go to heaven, or that his or her spirit becomes someone or something else. Others believe that nothing happens after the body stops working.

People have many different beliefs about death. There is no "right" or "wrong" way to believe.

If you have questions about what happens after someone dies, you can write about them.

....

....

....

....

You can ask someone in your family, a friend, or a religious leader about what they believe and write it down here:

....

....

....

....

Here, you can write down what you believe happens to people after they die.

....

....

....

....

What will change?

Sometimes when a person you love dies, things around you may change. Changes can be hard to get used to. You might be worried about what will change in your life, and you might have a lot of questions.

You can write your questions here:

....

....

....

....

What will stay the same?

It might make you feel better to know all of the things that WON'T change. Can you think of some things that you are happy will stay the same?

Write them here:

....

....

....

....

Other Questions

Below are some other questions that people sometimes ask after someone they love dies.

If you are wondering about any of these questions, you can write about it in your journal or talk to someone.

Why did they die?

Will they remember me?

Why did they leave me?

Can they hear me?

Will other people leave me?

Can they see me?

HOW WILL THINGS BE THE SAME WITHOUT THEM?

Will I ever see them again?

Are they in pain?

WHAT HAPPENS TO THEIR BODY?

Why them? Why me?

REMEMBERING
the Person You
LOVE

Talking about someone who died will help him or her stay in your heart and in your memory forever.

No matter where the road of your life takes you, the person who died will go with you because their memory will live on in your heart.

Turn the page to think more about the person you love and to make a scrapbook that shows how special he or she is to you!

Write down some things that you really love about the person who died.

Sometimes people we love do things that upset us.

It's OK if you sometimes got mad at the person who died. Maybe you even feel mad about their death. Here, you can write about something that he or she did that upset you:

What did he or she love about you?

People can make us feel very special by showing us or telling us how great they think we are. What are some of the things that this person loved about you?

What did you do that made him or her happy?

It feels great to make people happy, and you probably made this person happy in many different ways! Write about some of the ways here:

How are you alike?

Sometimes it is nice to think about how you are similar to the people you love. Maybe you look like them, act like them, or have some of their talents.

How are you similar to the person who died?

....

....

....

....

....

....

How are you different?

No two people are exactly alike— which is great because this is what makes us all unique and special.

What are the ways that you think you are different from him or her?

....

....

....

....

....

....

What are the ways you wish you were more like him or her?

....

....

....

....

More wonderful things...

What are some of the things that this person did that made you feel happy, warm, and great?

....

....

....

....

....

What did he or she teach you?

The people in our lives teach us things all the time, like how to read, play a game, cook a special meal, and lots and lots of other things.

Write down some of the things that this person taught you:

....

....

....

....

Special Memories

You probably have many memories about this person!

A Funny Memory

Write down a funny story that happened when you were together with him or her:

....

....

....

....

....

....

A Loving Memory

Think about a great day or some very special time you spent with him or her, and write about it here:

....

....

....

....

....

....

More Memories

Use this page to write about other memories you have of this special person.
You can come back to this page anytime and record even more memories!

Remembering Details

It can be comforting to remember little details about the person you love.

Fill in the blanks below. If you don't know an answer,
ask someone in your family or a friend for help.

Information about:
....
(Write his/her name above)

Date of birth:
....

Place of birth:
....

Eye color:
....

Hair color:
....

Parents' names:
....

....

Languages spoken:
....

Here, you can write about some of his or her favorite things:

Favorite food:

Favorite friends:

Favorite song:

Favorite place:

Favorite game:

Favorite hobby:

Favorite book:

Favorite piece of clothing or jewelry:

Favorite sport:

Favorite movie or tv show:

Favorite joke or story:

What are some of his or her other "favorites"?

Other Special Things to Remember

You probably know and remember a lot of other things about this person!

Here, you can write down some of your favorite details about him or her.
For example: did he or she have a special smile you can draw?
A special smell you can describe? A SPECIAL NICKNAME FOR YOU?
A funny expression he or she always said?

You can write about these, or other unique things here:

Great Advice He or She Gave You

....

....

....

....

....

A Secret You Shared

....

....

....

....

....

A Trip or Adventure

....

....

....

....

....

Draw a Picture

Use this page to draw a picture that reminds you of the person who died.
It could be a picture of the two of you or a picture of a special day you had together.

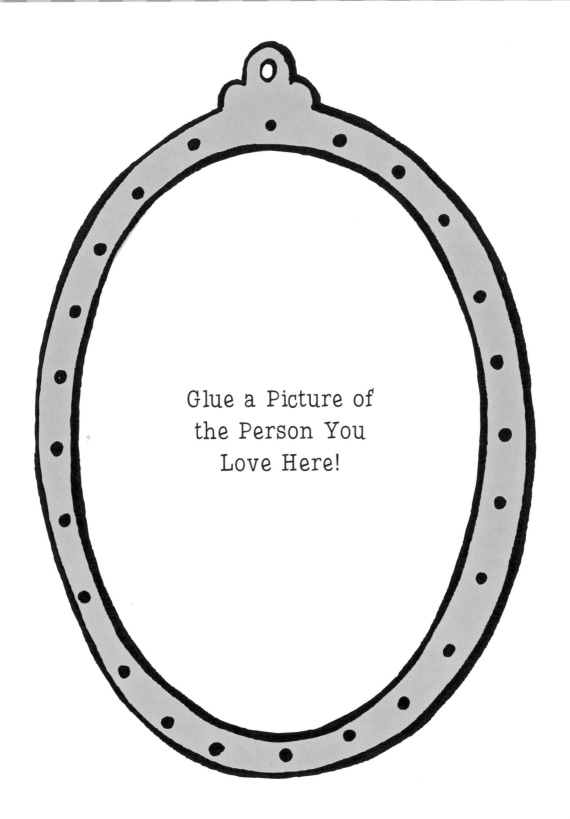

Glue a Picture of
the Person You
Love Here!

This person is a special part of your life, so you will never forget him or her!

Some Ways to
FEEL BETTER

Sometimes just thinking about special memories can make you feel better. It helps to remember that this person will always be a part of you through your memories.

There are also other things that you can do to feel better when you are sad or upset.

- Say a prayer
- Practice something he or she taught you
- Make a new friend
- Talk about him or her
- Learn something new
- Look at his or her picture
- Name a pet or stuffed animal after the person

Remember, everyone grieves differently. Some ideas might feel good to you—and others might not.

Turn the page for more ideas about ways to feel better. • • • • ▶

Talk to someone when you feel sad.

Family, friends, teachers, and therapists can listen when you want to talk.

Even other people who are sad about the death can help, too.
Don't worry, it won't make them more sad to talk to you.

Who do you like to talk to when you are sad?

Write down some of the things that people have said to you that have made you feel better. Then, when you are feeling upset you can read this page and remember the comforting things people have said to you.

Talk to the person who died.

Sometimes it helps to talk to the person who died—even if they can't talk back.

If you could talk to him or her now, what would you say?

....

....

....

....

....

....

....

Let your friends help.

When you are having a hard time, you might feel like your friends don't understand you. It's not that they don't care—maybe they just don't know what to say or how to act around you.

Even when it seems like they aren't saying or doing things that help, remember that your friends care about you.

If you want, you can try to explain how you are feeling to your friends. You can even tell them how they can help make you feel better.

Think about some of the things you did that made the person who died proud of you, and then keep doing those things.

What are some things you can do that would make him or her proud of you?

Honor the person on special days.

People can feel especially sad about their loss during holidays, birthdays, or other special days. Some people find it helpful to set aside some time on those days to remember the person who died. They might talk about the person, light a candle for them, draw a picture, or visit a special place that reminds them of the person who died.

If you feel extra-sad on special dates, that's totally normal.

Think about some things you can do on those days that might feel good to you.

Think about the other people who love you.

When someone dies, you might feel lonely or scared. Remember that there are many people who love you. Write down the names of some of the people who care about you:

Do something nice for someone else.

Sometimes doing something kind for someone else can make you feel better. If someone you know is also sad about the death, you can do nice things for him or her—like chores or making a special "feel better" card to spread some love. You can also do kind things for people you don't know. For example, you can donate money or time to an organization that your loved one cared about—or one that you think he or she would have liked.

Write down some things that you can do to make someone else feel good:

....

....

....

....

....

....

Do something nice for yourself.

Feeling upset and having things change can be stressful and tiring. Sometimes, it's good to take a break and do something really nice for yourself. Maybe you have a hobby or an activity that makes you feel relaxed and happy. Maybe there is a place you like to go or a friend you like to see that makes you feel better.

Think about some things you enjoy doing, and then don't forget to do them!

Make a special memory box.

Sometimes it feels good to look at things that remind you of the person who died. You might have special things that he or she gave to you that you like to look at, hold, or wear sometimes. You can even create a memory box and fill it with special things that remind you of him or her.

Can you think of some things that you might want to put in a memory box?

Create something to honor the person you love.

Sometimes people express their feelings by creating something in honor of the person who died. You could plant a tree and watch it grow. You could write a story about the person and then give it to other people who loved him or her. If the person taught you something special, you could teach it to someone else and pass along that skill. You can probably think of other special ways that you want to honor the person you lost.

Write a letter.

Some days, you might miss the person who died a lot, and you might want to tell him or her about your day or your feelings and thoughts. Whenever you feel like it, you can write a letter to him or her. You can start with this one:

Dear _____,

_____

_____

_____

_____

_____

_____

_____

_____

_____

From, _____

There's more to say?

Sometimes after people die, we wish we could have said a few last things to them.
Maybe you'd like to tell that person how much you admire him or her?
Or maybe you wish you could say "I love you" one more time. Even though he
or she probably knew how you feel, it can still be nice to get your feelings out.

Is there something you wish you could have said? You can write it here:

What would he or she say to you to help you feel better today?

Maybe the person who died is someone who would cheer you up when you were sad.
What do you think that person would say to you now to make you feel better?

"

"

EXPRESS Yourself

Your HEALING JOURNAL and SCRAPBOOK

We're leaving the next couple of pages blank for you.

Here's why: We know we didn't think of everything. You probably have other ideas about how to use these pages!

You can:

Fill these pages with photos or drawings of the person you love.

Write a story or poem about the person who died.

Make a collage of things that remind you of him or her.

Describe some of your favorite days that you spent with this person.

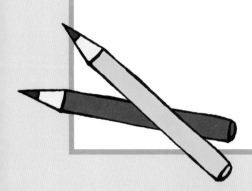

The HEALING BOOK BADGE
Be proud of yourself!

Expressing your feelings
after someone dies can be hard
and it takes a lot of strength.

You've done a great job of
remembering the person you love
and celebrating his or her life!

You've created a beautiful
book filled with memories.

You should be
proud of yourself
for your courage!

Reference Ideas

The Internet:

The Internet offers a wide range of resources on topics related to death, coping with change, and expressing feelings. Do a search using key words such as "kids and grief" or "kids and mourning" for more information.

Community resources:

You can find grief support resources in your community. Start by asking someone at your local hospital, church/temple, funeral home, or community center. There are bereavement centers (sometimes referred to as "grief centers" or "grief programs") throughout the country. School counselors may also know of resources.

Suggested reading:

There are many books for adults who are helping children to cope with death and for children who are facing the grieving process. Since new titles are offered regularly, check the Internet or ask a professional for the best current titles for your needs.

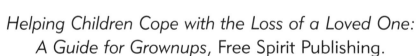

Some suggested reading for adults who are helping children to cope with death:

Helping Children Cope with the Loss of a Loved One: A Guide for Grownups, Free Spirit Publishing.

35 Ways to Help a Grieving Child, The Dougy Center

Share **THE HEALING BOOK**

Go to www.wateringcanpress.com to:

- Order additional books for children you know or to donate to an organization of your choice.

- Learn about bulk purchases for grieving centers, churches/temples, schools, or organizations.

- See other Watering Can® series books.

  The Giving Book: Open the Door to a Lifetime of Giving

  The Hero Book: Learning Lessons from the People You Admire

  The Autism Acceptance Book: Being a Friend to Someone with Autism

One of the ideas this book gives for feeling better involves doing nice things for other people. Here's an exciting way to feel good, help others, and give back!

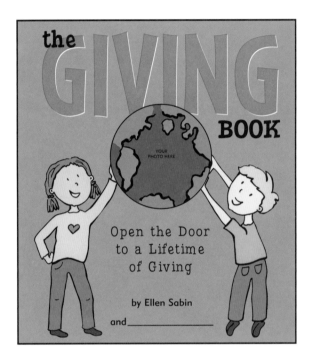

the GIVING BOOK

YOUR PHOTO HERE

Open the Door to a Lifetime of Giving

by Ellen Sabin

and _____

The GIVING BOOK is a really fun way to…

- Think about your wishes and dreams for making the world a better place!

- Appreciate how you feel when people are kind and giving to you.

- List all the different things you have to share with other people, like your talents, your time, and the things you have.

- Do fun activities with your family or friends to help other people. You can even do things to help animals or the planet.

- Learn ways to save money to give to your favorite charities or organizations.

- Realize how powerful your actions can be and how much of a difference you can make in the world!

The **GIVING BOOK** grows kids with character.

It is an activity book, a journal, and a scrapbook that inspires and records a child's journey into a lifelong tradition of giving and charity.

You've spent time thinking about the things you admire in someone you love. Now, you can think about even more people you value.

The HERO BOOK lets you think about the people you admire and the things that make you a hero, too!

The HERO BOOK lets you:

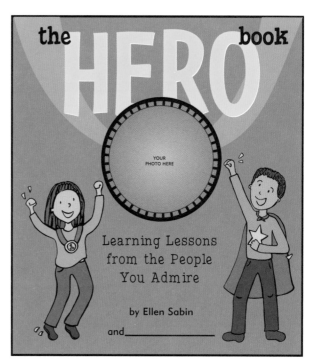

- Consider the qualities you admire in others.

- Write stories about people who show admirable traits like courage, fairness, or acts of kindness.

- Think about well-known heroes from history or everyday heroes from your own life.

- Write about what you learn from your role models.

- Think about the things that make you a hero to others!

The HERO BOOK grows kids with character.

It is an activity book, a journal, and a conversation-starter that sparks and records a child's journey into finding role models who will inspire them to be their best.

The Giving Book and The Hero Book are offered with free teacher's guides for use in classrooms. Free guides are also available for parents, youth groups, or others to use with the books in social settings. Find these free resources at www.wateringcanpress.com.

We hope that you always carry
with you wonderful, warm,
and loving thoughts about
the people you love.